Grace

Brides of Montana
Book Two

Cheryl Wright

Grace

Brides of Montana – Book Two

Copyright ©2020

by Cheryl Wright

Small Town Romance Publications

Dedication

To Margaret Tanner, my very dear friend and fellow author, for her enduring encouragement and friendship.

To Alan, my husband of over forty-nine years, who has been a relentless supporter of my writing and dreams for many years.

To You, my wonderful readers, who encourage me to continue writing these stories. It is such a joy knowing so many of you enjoy reading my stories as much as I love writing them for you.

Table of Contents

Chapter One

Grand Falls, Montana - 1880

Grace Sunderland straightened her back and braced for the jolt as the stage coach came to a sudden stop.

She glared at the work-weary cowboy sitting opposite. He'd ogled her since he joined them yesterday. She prayed he didn't alight here as well. She didn't need that.

Grand Falls promised to be the opportunity she sought. Business had never really been anything to write home about, but when her shop burned to the ground, it had been the sign she'd been waiting for.

It was definitely time to move on.

Grand Falls was said to be the place to be in for an upcoming business. It was expanding at a rapid rate, and Grace wanted to cash in on that.

She glanced around while the driver removed her trunk. Patrick Harper promised her would meet her here with the keys to her new home.

It was also her shop. She'd instructed him to build a small residence at the back. That had saved her quite a bit of money. And God only knew she didn't have much to spare.

The insurance payout was low. Based on her most recent sales record, they deemed not to pay her as much as she'd expected.

Thankfully Grace had managed to pull her sewing machine from the fire before it took hold. She also managed to rescue several bolts of fabric, some lace, and unfortunately, her sales records.

If the latter had perished, she may have received a better payout.

But it wasn't to be, and she'd decided to stop admonishing herself for what was done. She had a lot to look forward to, and that was exactly what she planned to do.

"Miss Sunderland?" The tall young man looked far too young to be her builder, but he held a set of keys in his hands, so she guessed it must be him.

She slowly turned to face him and planted a false smile on her face. "That is me. Mr Harper? Nice to finally meet you."

He stared at the trunk sitting at her feet. "Is this yours?" He snatched it up before she had a chance to answer, and carried it like it was a loaf of bread. She supposed building houses made you strong.

"Follow me, Miss Sunderland. Your shop is completely ready."

Grace nodded. She hadn't expected the shop to be ready since she'd arrived earlier than anticipated, so was pleasantly surprised.

"So the residence is fully furnished? Linens, crockery, cutlery..."

He glanced sideways at her. "Everything you requested is done. My wife assisted with outfitting the house once I was done."

His wife. What a pity. Not that she was looking for marriage, because she wasn't, but in a place like this, most probably the men would be like Patrick Harper – married and unavailable.

"My tools of trade are in that trunk, Mr Harper. So please be careful when you put it down."

His eyebrows rose in surprise. "This is everything? I thought you would have more."

"The fire destroyed practically everything," she said quietly. "I was lucky to get these out."

The memory of that day flooded her senses.

She'd lost everything that meant anything to her, including her constant companion. Her six-year-old cat Grumps, named due to his mood swings, had been in the residence when the fire broke out.

Grace had never allowed him in the shop – she couldn't afford to have customers complain about cat fur on their purchases. Sadness suddenly overwhelmed her. She had believed him to be out of the house, and when she discovered he wasn't, she tried her hardest to get him out. Flames lapped about her, and concerned bystanders held her back.

She'd fought against them, but by the time she broke free it was far too late. Grumps was gone.

"Here we are," he said unexpectedly, pulling her out of her miserable thoughts. He handed over the keys and she unlocked the door.

Standing in the doorway, she glanced about. It looked good. Empty of course, but well made. She expected nothing less. Patrick Harper had come highly recommended, and she was certain he wouldn't let her down.

Clutching her carpetbag, Grace gingerly took a few steps inside. Her eyes took in the shelves around the small room, exactly as she'd requested. The cupboards along the back wall, and the larger room separate from the shop. That was where she would do her work, and it was far larger than the shop itself.

The shop was merely a display area.

She'd sent the layout to Patrick – this store was an exact replica of the one she lost.

It would be some days before she could open the doors. Grace had ordered fabric, as well as models on which to display her wares.

Her eyes scanned the room as she imagined where everything would go.

Grace took a deep restorative breath, then slowly let it out. This was the beginning of her new life. A life she hoped would be better than the last one.

* * *

Joe Harkley stared out the window of his store.

His tailor shop stood almost directly opposite the new store Patrick had been building. It wasn't until the sign had been painted on the window he knew what kind of store it would be.

Then he'd smiled.

Finally a storekeeper he could work with.

Graceful Bonnets

Proprietor G. Sunderland

He'd watched as the words had been added in gold paint. Clearly this would be good for them both. He would give Mr Sunderland time to settle in, then would wander over and introduce himself.

At the very least they could recommend each other's services. At best, they could work in unison and ensure their customers had a completely co-ordinated outfit.

Yes, Joe liked the thought of that. Things had been a little slow lately, but business was picking up.

With the influx of families, orders were starting to roll in more regularly. The ladies in particular graced his store most often. Men's suits were rather expensive these days, so the men of the town often made do with what they had.

Of course there would always be customers who preferred to buy off the shelf at the Mercantile.

That thought sparked an idea. Perhaps he should have some ready-made outfits – both men's and women's – and have them on display should a customer come looking.

That would have to be the best idea he'd had for a long time. Perhaps Mr Sunderland would make some bonnets to match. That way they would both win.

He nodded his head in satisfaction then turned back to his current project.

* * *

Grace pulled her best gown from the wardrobe.

She hadn't brought much with her, because most of her belongings perished in the fire. She decided to wait until she got to Grand Falls before replacing them.

She'd had the best sleep last night, and would be forever grateful for Patrick and his wife Emily for ensuring her home was fully equipped and furnished.

She dressed then sat at the dresser brushing her long gold drenched hair. On workdays, she pulled it up into a chiffon, but other times she liked it to hang down over her shoulder.

Today she tied it up in a ponytail, with much of it hanging loose.

Her heart fluttered at the thought of her first time at the Grand Falls church. She knew no-one here except Patrick Harper. She wasn't much good with people she didn't know, but hoped she would soon settle in.

She sat at the small table in her kitchen and sipped the weak tea she'd made. Grace had never been one for coffee – couldn't stand the bitter taste. Even adding sugar hadn't helped.

Her parents had never approved of her line of business, stating it was fraught with danger. Mostly the danger of not having customers. Not that she would ever admit it, but they were right.

She didn't know if it was where she'd decided to open her store, or the nature of the business. Little Rock was far too small; she'd realized after a few months of opening there, but by then it was too late.

She'd put most of her savings into not only moving there, but establishing the store itself.

The insurance payout from the fire helped to establish this place, but would not carry her for long. If Grand Falls didn't work out, Grace had no idea what she would do.

At least she had a home, and the work Patrick had done was fully paid, so she would survive the next few weeks at least. Thankfully her fabric orders were paid as well.

Perhaps she was better off than she realized.

Grace carried her cup to the sink then rinsed and dried it.

It was past time she left for church. She didn't want to be late her first time there. The last thing she wanted was for people to see her as tardy.

That could leave her with a reputation as a poor business woman, and she was far from that.

She snatched up her bonnet and placed it on her head, glancing in the mirror to ensure it was on straight.

Grace stepped out of the door to her residence, and breathed in the fresh air. What she'd seen of Grand Falls so far was lovely. The air was clean, and it was quiet here.

She loved that part already. Now to meet the people; she hoped they were equally nice.

She wandered down Main Street, glancing at the variety of stores. Everything was closed, being Sunday, but later she would have a good look around.

Tomorrow she would open the door to her new store for the first time. But for now, she would head toward the church. She hoped it would become a place of refuge for her. Somewhere she could go and feel... safe.

Not that she was in danger, but her heart had taken a big hit when she'd lost Grumps. He had been her constant companion, and she missed him dearly.

Lost in her thoughts, Grace almost collided with a gent who was also walking toward the church. She smiled at him, but neither of them said a word.

Not immediately at least.

"You're new here," he said, startling her.

She looked him up and down. He was very well dressed, and his suit was of the highest standard. Probably the best she'd ever seen.

Being a seamstress herself, she could see the quality of the garment. "I am," she said gracefully. "I arrived a few days ago."

He reached out his hand and Grace accepted it. "I'm Joe," he said, his eyes rolling over her gown. She wondered if he was doing it in spite because of her own leisurely examination.

"Grace." She tripped on a crack in the path, and he grabbed her arm to stop her falling.

He held tight until they reached the bottom. "Are you alright?" he asked, concern in his voice.

She was shaken, but not hurt, and nodded to tell him so. She took a restorative breath. "Thank you," she said. "I would have looked a muddle turning up to my first day at the Grand Falls church in a soiled gown."

He grinned and a tingle shot down her spine. He had seemed quite stern until that moment, and she wished he would smile more.

He probably thought the same of her.

Joe guided her toward the hallowed building, but she really didn't need his guidance. She could see the steeple from way back, and would follow her instincts.

Her heart thudded when she saw the holy structure, emotion overwhelming her. It had been a while since she'd been to church, what with the fire then ending up homeless until she was able to get her insurance sorted.

Thank goodness for her Aunt Mary who had discovered her predicament and taken her in.

Finally Grace felt she'd outlived her welcome, or at least she was worried she would, and made plans to leave.

Once her insurance money arrived, she set her plans in place.

As she looked around the church, she felt completely at home, and took a seat in the back of the room.

She reached for a bible, and quietly read the comforting words while she waited for the service to begin. At the first notes of the organ, she glanced up, and saw Patrick Harper and his young family a few pews further down.

Soon the music stopped and the preacher spoke. "Good morning everyone." He had a huge smile on his face, and she immediately warmed to him. "I can see at least one unfamiliar face." Grace felt her cheeks heat. "I am Preacher Angus Devon, and I would like to welcome you to our humble service."

There was a pause, and then he spoke again. "Let us begin by bowing our heads in prayer."

The more Grace was in this place, the more at home she felt. It was as though she was surrounded by love.

That was such a silly notion, she admonished herself. She didn't know these people and they didn't know her.

Perhaps in a few weeks that feeling would be justified, but certainly not now.

She stood when a hymn was introduced, and sang along with the rest of the congregation. The service was ended with The Lord's Prayer, which she recited along with everyone else.

Preacher Devon headed to the entrance and spoke to everyone as they left. His face brightened when it was finally her turn. "Good morning! Welcome to our church family," he said, sounding very happy to see her."

"That was a lovely service," she said. "Thank you for the warm welcome. I'm Grace Sunderland. I moved to Great Falls a few days ago."

"Your name seems familiar?" He seemed to study her more closely. "Oh, I think I remember. You've opened a new store in town, I think."

She grinned. "I have. Tomorrow is opening day, so fingers crossed."

"You own *Graceful Bonnets*?"

Joe's voice behind her startled Grace. She turned to face him. "I certainly do. Let's hope the bonnet business around here is good."

"We need to talk." She frowned at his words, but stood aside and waited.

She was soon accosted by an older lady. "Welcome my dear," the woman said. "I am Edna Baker. I own the diner in town."

Mrs Baker led Grace to the church hall where they could have a hot beverage and get to know each other, she'd said.

Grace did not refuse.

She knew Grand Falls was not a huge town, but it was evolving, and with it would come new customers. That's what she needed. Little Rock was not expanding, so her business options were very limited.

As the two woman sat chatting in the back corner of the hall, Grace felt even more at home. Mrs Baker was lovely, and Grace felt as though she'd know her all her life.

How wonderful would it be to have that sort of bright personality. She was the complete opposite.

"Good morning, Mrs Baker." It was Joe – he stood in front of the two of them expectantly. "Might I have a word with Miss Sunderland?"

"Of course." Mrs Baker graciously stood, letting Joe take her place. "If you need anything, you come and see me at the diner," she said, patting Grace's hand.

She was quickly on her way and soon chatting with other parishioners.

Grace took a deep breath. What could this stranger want with her? She turned to him and smiled tentatively.

"Miss Sunderland," he said gently. "Let me properly introduce myself – I am Joe Harkley. I had no idea who you were when we met earlier this morning."

She was confused. Grace had introduced herself.

"I was expecting a man," he continued. "The signage said G. Sunderland, and naturally I assumed a male."

She blinked slowly then stared at him. *A man? Why would he assume such a thing?* "I don't understand Mr Harkley. Why would you think I am a man?"

She stood and twirled about. "Do I look like a man to you?" She smiled slyly and he laughed.

"My dear Miss Sunderland," he said, a grin on his face. "You are the farthest from a man as I could wish for."

"Then..."

"My tailor shop is opposite yours," he explained. "I thought perhaps we could work together. Help each other."

Her business brain had switched on. "In what way, Mr Harkley?"

She took a sip of her tea, and stared over her cup at him. She listened very carefully to what Mr Harkley had to say.

Chapter Two

Joe stared at Grace over his mug of coffee.

Mrs Baker had graciously allowed them to discuss their business dealings in her diner. They couldn't go to his store alone, and the same applied to her store and residence.

It was quite a dilemma until dear Mrs Baker had spoken up. Joe was sure that woman had the keenest of hearing!

So here they sat, in the quiet of the diner. It was far too early for the diner crowd to arrive, and the establishment had only just opened for the day.

The added bonus was the coffee was the best in town.

"What do you think?" He glanced at Grace, trying not to stare. She was a pretty young woman – far too young to be running a business in his opinion.

Joe wondered why she hadn't been married off by now. She seemed like a nice person. But then ambition often got in the way with some of these women folk.

He sighed. What was it about this generation that put crazy thoughts in their heads. He inwardly shook himself. None of his business.

She placed her mug of tea on the coaster in front of her and swallowed. "Let me make sure I understand. When you get an order for a gown, you will recommend the customer crosses the road and gets an appropriate bonnet from me."

She frowned.

"Or... you will convince the customer she needs a matching bonnet, and we will work together to ensure that happens."

She stared at him.

Was it such a crazy idea? He didn't think so.

She leaned forward and put her elbows on the table. Joe was horrified – women who had been brought up properly did not do such a thing!

"What's in it for you?" Her words demanded an answer.

There wasn't a lot, he must admit. "You could recommend your customers to me if they require gowns?"

She leaned back, and he felt a little more comfortable. He hadn't expected her to question him at all.

She looked thoughtful, then shook her head. She took a sip of tea, then smiled. "We could have some brochures printed," she said thoughtfully.

"Yours advertising your bonnets," he said. "And mine advertising..."

She leaned in again. "No, that won't work. We need something a bit more... innovative." She tapped her fingers on the table, then lifted her hand for Mrs Baker to come over.

"Mrs Baker," she said when the woman arrived. "If you wanted a gown and a matching bonnet, would you rather go to one store or two?"

She didn't hesitate. "Why, one of course. I'd rather not waste my time going to two different stores."

"Thank you," Grace said with a grin.

He finally saw where her thoughts were going. The question was, how did they manage that when they had two different stores?

"I noticed, when we walked past your store on our way here," she said. "You had some pre-made gowns. Do you have any of the fabric left?"

He nodded.

"Enough for a bonnet?"

He nodded again. "I guess so."

"Then shall we come to an agreement on a price, and you can sell your pre-made co-ordinated outfit?"

He raised his eyebrows. "Brilliant idea!" he almost shouted. Then he paused, deflated. "What if I can't sell either?"

"You won't have to pay me until the outfit is sold. Fair enough?"

He rubbed his hands together. "That is more than fair."

They spent the rest of their time together working on their advertising brochure. They would ask Cecil Delbert from the Mercantile to put a brochure in his store window except that would be in complete competition to his own products.

Perhaps they could leave a pile at the post office? And maybe Mrs Baker would be willing to help as well.

Joe had a good feeling about this arrangement. It's a pity Miss Sunderland was a woman, but he could work with that.

* * *

Grace sat at her precious sewing machine.

She had bought it in Helena when a notorious sweat-shop had finally been closed down by the local government. They'd broken so many laws, and lives had been put at risk.

It had cost her a small fortune, but it had been worth it.

Grace couldn't begin to count the number of bonnets she'd made on this little beauty.

She looked down at the treadle. The once-shiny black paint was beginning to peel, but it was a miracle it had survived the fire.

If she hadn't rushed in and dragged it out, she wouldn't have it now.

She swallowed. If she hadn't wasted precious time retrieving her sewing machine, her beautiful feline companion would be at her feet right now.

Tears stung the back of her eyes, but she had to push through. She promised Mr Harkley she would have four bonnets ready for him to add to his display by tomorrow evening. That was perhaps a foolish promise to make.

It would be a push, but provided she stuck to her schedule, it was very doable.

He'd told her not to rush, but this was far too good an opportunity to let it pass her by. Grace glanced at the pile of excess fabric Mr Harkley had provided. There was enough material and then some for each bonnet to make it a matching outfit.

She was cutting the strings of cotton from the first bonnet when the bell over the door tingled.

"Good morning," she called as she left her machine. "I am Grace Sunderland. How may I help you?"

"Good morning," the older woman said, wholly animated. "I am very excited at such a wonderful addition to our town." She stepped forward and pulled Grace into her warm embrace, then suddenly pushed back. "Oh! I do apologize – I haven't introduced myself. Esther Davis."

She stood there and stared as though she was waiting for Grace to say something.

"Well my dear," she said when no words were forthcoming from Grace. "I am in need of a new bonnet. My dear friend Mrs Baker said you make beautiful bonnets."

Grace had to force herself not to grin at the words. The only bonnet Mrs Baker had seen of hers was the one Grace had worn to church. Still, it was never good to refuse business.

"I must thank Mrs Baker for her kind words," Grace said, and meant it. "I have a few bonnets on display, or custom made is also an option."

Mrs Davis stared at her. "Custom made. Mr Davis would have kittens if I arrived home with something ready made." Her lips curled. "He is such a snob. It comes from having far too much money."

Grace couldn't help it – she raised her eyebrows, and Mrs Davis laughed.

She hooked her arm through Grace's and began to stroll through the tiny store studying each of the fabrics on display. She stopped at a bolt of the highest quality cotton. It was beige in color and had tiny pink flowers on it.

Grace had balked at the price, but had been assured it was popular. Especially with the wealthy ladies.

"This one," she said, touching the fabric to her cheek. "I'd like a gown with a matching bonnet," she demanded in the nicest possible way.

"I don't make gowns, but between us, Mr Harkley and myself can fulfill your order."

Mrs Davis gave her the biggest smile. "That's wonderful, Grace. Let's look for additional fabric. As you can see, my wardrobe desperately needs refreshing."

Grace could see no such thing, but had no intentions of informing her first, and possibly her best customer that she was completely wrong.

* * *

Miss Sunderland had agreed to meet with Joe in a few days, but here she was already. She surely couldn't be finished the four bonnets already?

She stood in the middle of his store and glanced about, perusing his wares. "Good morning, Miss Sunderland," he said brightly. "What can I do for you?"

"It seems our arrangement has already gleaned some attention."

Before she could answer, Joe intervened. "How so?" His curiosity got the better of him.

"Mrs Davis has ordered a new wardrobe of clothes with matching bonnets." She grinned, and his heart thudded. "She has chosen her fabrics from my store. She said you have her measurements and know what she likes."

Joe rubbed his hands together. "You know what this means?"

She stared curiously at him. "No, I have no idea."

Of course, she was new in town. "Mr Davis is the richest man for miles around. Mrs Davis likes clothes. She is also generous with her recommendations." He grinned broadly, he couldn't help himself.

He strode toward the front door of his store and turned a sign around. It said *back in ten minutes*. Joe hoped he would be, but if not, it wouldn't be much longer.

Grace followed him out and he locked the door, then hooked her arm through his. They then crossed the road together.

"Once word gets around, we'll both be very busy."

She stared at him. "But if she's rich and others aren't...."

"They won't care," he said. "Emulating Mrs Davis is a favorite pastime for some of the local women."

"I see," Grace said, the faintest hint of a smile on her face.

"You're not happy?" She seemed happy with their arrangement, but now? He wasn't so sure.

"It, it's a lot of pressure," she said quietly. "I've only ever made bonnets for regular people before, not rich women."

Her words made him laugh, but that in turn produced a frown from her. "Pretend Mrs Davis is a regular person, then." There was a hint of mockery in his words, and he wondered if Grace realized.

She stared at him then pouted. "I don't appreciate you mocking me, Mr Harkley," she said, then pulled away from him and unlocked the door to her store. She stormed off toward her fabric displays and proceeded to show him the choices Mrs Davis had made.

He could have predicted most of them, as he'd been outfitting Mrs Davis for a long time, and his father before him.

"They are rather beautiful fabrics," Joe said, rubbing the fabrics between his fingers. "Good quality too. We need to sit down together and work out a fair price for both of us."

Grace didn't respond and he worried she'd quoted a price already. "Did you give Mrs Davis a price, Miss Sunderland?" he asked quietly.

She glared at him. "Of course not! Besides, she said price is no object – just make up her order and bill her husband."

"Excellent." Mrs Davis was Joe's favorite customer. She left everything to him, and she was willing to pay a little more to get the best available. "Take what you need for the bonnets, then give me the rest. Once I have what I need, I'll return the rest."

She reached for her scissors. "Have you used any of these fabrics here in Grand Falls?" He studied her face, and she looked uncomfortable.

"No, not yet."

"Then don't. It is now redundant. Mr Davis does not enjoy seeing other woman parade around in the same fabric as his wife's."

Her eyes opened wide. "But..."

"No buts. You can sell it out of town, far away from Grand Falls. To another seamstress perhaps but not locally. You will be paid handsomely for it, so do not upset yourself."

Her relief was palpable, and Joe felt suddenly elated for her. He had the distinct impression Grace Sunderland had not been appreciated wherever she was located previously.

He hoped that was about to change.

"I will work out all the costings, if you will allow me." She looked rather displeased. "I promise you will be handsomely rewarded."

He glanced about at the bonnets she had on display, and lifted the price tags. "You will get three times this amount for your custom bonnets from Mrs Davis."

Grace gasped. "Isn't that dishonest?" she asked. "Just because she's rich..."

He stopped her mid-sentence. "It's because she's rich that she is able to demand such unreasonable conditions. Do not concern yourself, Grace. This is a business arrangement I have with Mr Davis."

Once Grace had taken the amount of fabric she needed, she put seven bolts of fabric in her sewing room, out of sight.

Joe grabbed two and headed for the door. "I'll return shortly for the rest. I have more storage space than you do." She opened the door for him, and he stepped outside, but suddenly turned back. "Make this order a priority, Grace," he said gently. "As I will do. We don't want to get on Mr Davis's bad side."

He strolled to the other side of the road, and unlocked his store. He could feel her gaze on his back. Their business arrangement was off to an amazing start, but he was going to have to educate Grace on some of the more... delicate issues of this business.

Chapter Three

Grace was ecstatic and reluctant all at the same time.

She couldn't believe she had landed such a big order on the first day of opening her new store. And Mr Harkley... he was a Godsend.

What would she do without his guidance?

It was rather strange that Mrs Davis had come to her instead of Mr Harkley who knew her so well. Grace shook herself. She was overthinking things. Again.

She'd always been like that, according to her father. When she announced she would be a seamstress, he told her she was overthinking her future. *What woman needs a career?* he'd bellowed. *Women are meant to marry and bear children!*

It was useless arguing with him, so she simply stared, then left the room. She made her decision in those few moments.

She decided right then and there to leave home and make her own way in the world. It was hard to admit now, but perhaps her father had been right. She'd made a mess of things, and her entire livelihood had burned down. The worst of it was the death of her dear companion.

Grace wiped a stray tear from her cheek. *Would she never get over losing her precious feline?* She sat at her sewing machine, and finished the bonnet she'd begun earlier. It only needed the matching ribbon to be added and would be done – might as well finish it and get it out of the way.

Then she could begin work on the first of Mrs Davis's bonnets. She'd not long started when the bell over the door tinkled.

She looked up to see Mr Harkley filling the doorway.

Of course – he was back for more bolts of fabric.

As he brushed past her, she felt the slight breeze he caused, and a thrill went down her spine. Grace shook herself. *What a terribly strange reaction.*

"I'll return shortly," he said, and again was gone.

Grace looked down at her newest project. This bonnet would be very special. She would add ruffles to the brim, and would trim it with the most delicate of lace. The cap would be gathered with lace at the base, and be especially comfortable while looking as elegant as it could possibly be.

She decided against the traditional ribbon to tie it, and instead would use matching lace.

"That already looks amazing," Mr Harkley said, startling her out of her thoughts. She hadn't even heard him enter the store again. "Mrs Davis is going to love that."

"I certainly hope so," she said. "If she's paying me so much money, it has to be worth it."

His face went grim. *Had she spoken out of turn?* What she said was true – just because she was rich didn't mean Mrs Davis had to pay more.

He collected the last of the fabric, but instead of leaving he hovered beside her sewing machine. "It's her choice, you know. At least it's her husband's. Mrs Davis is not such a snob as he is."

She could feel his eyes on her, and glanced up at him. "I'm not sure what you mean."

Mr Harkley shifted from one foot to the other. "It's a long-time arrangement. We give her preference over other customers, and we get paid handsomely for it. I have all her measurements and she doesn't have to bother with fittings and such."

His fingers tapped the casing of the sewing cabinet.

"Was there something else, Mr Harkley?"

He glanced down at her and frowned. "No, I guess not. I'm sorry to have bothered you. I'll be on my way."

As the door closed behind him, Grace felt something come over her. It took a few minutes to realize it was aloneness.

She'd never encountered it before, not really. But the moment Mr Harkley left her store, she'd felt it – an emptiness that disappeared whenever he was near.

* * *

As she pulled the curtains closed on the store windows, she noticed a light still burned in Mr Harkley's store.

Surely he wasn't still working at this hour of the night? There was little enough light to do paperwork at night, let alone to make clothes, assuming that's what he was doing.

She stared for long moments, deciding whether to visit and ensure he was okay, but decided against it. Instead she settled on a short stroll. There was still some light left, and the moon sat high in the sky.

Besides, she wouldn't go far. She might even visit Mrs Baker's diner and have supper. It had been a long day and the last thing Grace felt like doing tonight was prepare food.

Yes, that's what she would do. Assuming she could get a table, that is.

She locked up the store and went through to the residence to freshen up. She looked herself up and down in the full-length mirror.

Not perfect, but not too bad either. She didn't feel like changing, and ran her hands down her slightly ruffled skirts.

She brushed out her hair and pulled it into a ponytail, then pulled on her bonnet and proceeded out onto the street.

Her residence opened out onto a small alleyway, and although it was perfectly fine by day, it felt a little scary at night.

There was rarely anyone else along here after dark. At least she presumed that was the case – she hadn't ventured out at night before. She shivered as she hurried along the cobbled path.

Relief flooded her as she turned onto the main street which was far more illuminated. As she crossed the street toward the diner, she spotted Mr Harkley locking up his store.

"Good evening, Mr Harkley," she said brightly. Seeing him was enough to put a spring in her step.

"Oh!" She startled him, but he didn't appear perturbed. "Good evening, Miss Sunderland."

"I'm on my way to the diner for supper. If there's a table, that is." She glanced in the direction of the diner but couldn't gauge the availability. "Would you care to join me?"

He flashed her a smile. "I would be delighted, Miss Sunderland. I was about to do the same – it's been a very long day." As if to prove the point, he stretched his back and arms then strolled toward her and extended his arm. "Shall we?"

Grace shuddered as they made contact. *What was it about this man that made her react every time they were near?*

She shook the thought aside. They hadn't known each other long enough for such feelings to occur. She turned to him and smiled gracefully. "Thank you, Mr Harkley."

He nodded and they headed to the diner, which was near empty as Mr Harkley said it would. Monday night was a quiet night for the diner, he said. Friday and Saturday nights were Mrs Baker's busy nights, and bookings were required for those.

"This is a pleasant surprise," Mrs Baker said as she greeted them both, then led them to a table near the window.

"Before I forget," Grace said cheerfully. "Thank you for recommending my bonnets to Mrs Davis.

The older woman's face brightened. "I guess that means she visited you. I'm so pleased."

She would never know what her recommendation meant to Grace. It could be the beginning of a long and fruitful business in this developing town.

Grace didn't expand on Mrs Davis's visit. She was sure the other woman wouldn't be pleased if she did. Eventually everyone would know when they saw her outfits, but for now, it would be their secret.

They placed their orders, and the two chatted about some of the aspects of their new 'partnership' and Mr Harkley told her a little about his business.

In return, she told him how her previous store had burned down. "The police were convinced it was arson," she said quietly. "But no one was ever arrested for it."

He reached across the table and patted her hand. "That's terrible," he said.

When she told him about Grumps, he was even more sympathetic. "I'm very sorry," he said gently.

The warmth of his hand was reassuring, but Grace gently pulled her hand away. What would people say? Besides, the thrill that ran down her spine at the contact was worrying.

She'd never had anything like this happen before. Was it normal when a man touched a woman for this sort of thing to occur? She would try to forget it for now.

The food arrived, and she was glad for the reprieve. No more talking, only eating. It was a much safer option.

"I'm far too full for dessert," Mr Harkley announced when Mrs Baker returned. "What about you, Miss Sunderland."

"I am the same. I shall go for a stroll to walk some of it off."

He looked horrified. "Oh my. You cannot go alone – not at this time of night."

She stared at him. She thought it would be safe here.

"I agree," Mrs Baker interjected. "Grand Falls is generally safe, but you just never know who is lurking around."

He stood, and she followed suit. "I shall accompany you," he said forcefully.

As much as she was annoyed at his presumption, she was looking forward to a nice stroll in the brisk evening air.

She balked when Mr Harkley insisted on paying for her meal. After all, she had planned to eat alone.

He won out in the end, after telling her she'd insulted him. He did wink as he said it, so Grace took it half-heartedly.

"Where would you like to go?" He offered her his arm and she accepted. "Mind the steps."

She hadn't even noticed and would have surely tripped. "I don't really care where we go. I just want to walk to stretch my back."

He grinned. "I am somewhat the same tonight. Shall we just stroll and see where the night takes us?"

She nodded and they were soon on their way. He pointed out some of the businesses along the way, several she would want to visit at some point. Like the Mercantile, the post office, and even the bank. She'd transferred her account here, but hadn't visited the bank manager yet.

That was a job for the near future.

"Does your back feel any better," he asked after they'd walked for about thirty minutes.

"Oh, it does, Mr Harkley. It really does. Thank you." And it did, but now it was time to go home. "I am feeling rather tired now, and will leave you to go home."

He frowned. "You must be joking. There is no way I would leave you to walk alone down that dark alleyway." He looked rather affronted. "I shall walk you to your door and see you are home safely."

"Why, thank you, Mr Harkley. I do appreciate it. I have to admit to feeling a little...dubious when I left tonight."

He patted her hand. "Think nothing of it, Miss Sunderland."

They made the rest of the trip in silence, which Grace appreciated. She was far to exhausted for chit-chat. But she enjoyed it nonetheless.

She unlocked the door and Mr Harkley told her he would wait until her door was locked behind her before he left. It was such a gentlemanly thing to do, but no one had ever bothered to do such a thing before.

It made her pause.

Chapter Four

After several days of making bonnets for Mrs Davis, Grace felt like she never wanted to sew another one.

It was at times frustrating, as she'd attempted to make each bonnet unique. She was sure her new customer would appreciate her extra effort. Besides, if she was being paid so much, she should ensure it was worth the money.

She placed the last of the bonnets in a hat box, and sat it on the top of the others. They were safe here, and also out of Mr Harkley's way.

He had been working hard on the gowns that matched her bonnets, but told her they would all be finished by the following weekend.

How he managed that she would never know.

Or perhaps she did.

Working late into the night would be one solution.

He was a grown man – he knew what he was doing. And Grace would love to be able to help him, as he had helped her. But alas, she did not have experience making gowns.

She needed a break from being bent over a sewing machine and decided to take a short stroll. She locked the door to the store and began to explore some of the other businesses.

First stop was the Mercantile where she introduced herself to Mr Delbert, the owner. Grace wandered around the store and came across a rack of gowns. They were very pretty, and she almost bought one.

But how would it look for a seamstress to go buying ready-made gowns? The least she should do is ask Mr Harkley to make one for her, but he was incredibly busy right now.

Should she attempt to make one herself? She had a nice array of fabrics to choose from.

The decision only took twenty seconds. She had never been much of a seamstress when it came to clothes. Bonnets had always been her forte. Grace had made hats before too, when requested, but wasn't convinced she could stitch a wearable gown.

No, she would ask Mr Harkley to refresh her wardrobe, as Mrs Davis had. Only in Grace's case, she only needed one or two gowns. She was far from being a socialite.

Next she visited the post office, where she introduced herself to Mr Abner Ackerman. If mail or a telegraph arrived for her, she needed to know it could be delivered.

She went to the butcher shop where she bought a small roast. Mr Dunning told her this piece of meat would be best put in the oven at lunchtime.

After leaving, a thought crossed her mind – it hardly seemed worth the effort to make a roast for herself, but perhaps Mr Harkley...

She shook the thought away. It wouldn't be proper, would it, having a man in her home? Alone.

Goodness, no. She couldn't do that.

She hurried back home with the meat in its wrapping, ready to go in the icebox until it was time to place it in the oven. She was very grateful Patrick Harper had thought of all the little things.

Or perhaps it was his wife, Emily. She smiled. Yes, it would definitely be his wife.

Either way, Grace was grateful for the essential amenities.

She dearly wanted to continue her amble around town, but needed to get back to work. She'd squandered enough of her time already.

"Ah, Miss Sunderland!" Mr Harkley hurried across the main street toward her. "Do you have a moment to spare?" He didn't wait for an answer but continue to hurry toward her.

She stared at him as she clutched her piece of beef, an indulgence if ever there was one.

"Good morning, Mr Harkley." She waited for him to reach her, wondering what all the fuss was about.

"I'm glad I caught you, Miss Sunderland," he said, seeming a little breathless having rushed across the road to reach her. "Do you have plans for Sunday?"

She closed her eyes in a slow blink. Of course she had plans. "I will be attending church. Of course." It was a forgone conclusion.

"I thought perhaps you could accompany me to the church picnic in the afternoon."

A slow smile came to her face. "How delightful," she said, dropping her package as she began to clap her hands in her excitement.

He caught it for her as he laughed.

"Oh dear, I'd totally forgotten about the piece of roast beef I'd bought."

His eyes opened wide. "It's a long time since I've had a roast," he explained. "It's hardly worth the effort for one. Are you having company?"

Before she could think, the words were out of her mouth. "I thought perhaps you would care to join me?"

"I, I wasn't vying for an invitation, Miss Sunderland." He backed off with his hands in front of him.

She reached out and grabbed his sleeve. "Please don't," she said. "I bought it with you in mind." It was the truth. She wouldn't mention the fact she was having second thoughts.

Her concern was leaving her reputation in tatters by entertaining a man in her home. The two of them alone.

Well, it was too late now. That horse had already bolted.

"In that case, I would be delighted, Miss Sunderland." He began to turn away, but suddenly turned back. "What can I bring? As a contribution to the meal?"

"No need," she said, but another thought struck her. "I do need a favor though."

His eyes slanted and he stared at her.

"Not now, but once you're done with Mrs Davis's order, I would like to order some gowns from you."

He frowned.

"Most of my belongings were destroyed in the fire. I thought of buying some from the Mercantile..."

"Please don't," he said quickly. "I can certainly accommodate you, make something especially for you."

"Thank you," she said, then turned to unlock the door. "Tonight at say, six?"

"Six it is." She heard him whistling as he strolled back across the road.

As bold as her invitation had been, even with her reservations, Grace was looking forward to this evening's meal.

* * *

Grace closed up early to attend to the evening meal. The last thing she wanted was to leave a bad impression on Joe Harkley.

After all, it was presumed all women could cook.

She'd been given instructions at the butcher's shop, so was confident the meat would be fine. At least she hoped it would be. She'd added the potatoes, onions, and carrots at the time Mr Dunning had also instructed.

She opened the oven door briefly – everything seemed to be fine. It smelled pretty good, so she closed the door again.

Grace had purchased fresh beans from the Mercantile, and prepared them earlier. They sat in the saucepan ready to cook.

She turned back to the counter and finished cutting the peeled apples. The pastry sat waiting to be rolled out.

Before she'd left, Aunt Mary had insisted Grace take her much loved and well-used recipe book. She'd balked at the time, but now she was incredibly grateful of Aunt Mary's determination. She wouldn't be standing here baking if it hadn't been for her aunt's thoughtfulness.

She wiped her hands across the white apron she wore, then tackled the apples once more. She'd never made apple pie before, and the task was daunting.

In fact, she'd never baked anything before, although she had helped Aunt Mary on several occasions.

The moment the pie was in the oven, she set about readying the table. She flicked a clean white cloth over the small table, and lay the cutlery perfectly, as her mother had taught her.

She placed a crimson linen napkin next to each fork, then set out a jug of water and two glasses.

The butter and bread had just been added to the table when there was a knock at her door.

"No, no, no!" she said under her breath. "I'm not ready – he can't be here yet." But she knew he was.

She took a deep breath and headed toward the door, opening it a crack.

He took one look at her and grinned. "Good evening, Miss Sunderland," he said cheerfully.

He might change his mind when he tastes the food, she thought ruefully. She was certain he had no idea what he was getting into.

She opened the door wide and he stepped inside. "Welcome to my humble abode." She took his jacket and hat, and hung them up on the coat rack that sat next to the front door. She tried to sound normal, joyful, but inside she felt all sorts of anxiety.

He glanced about. "You have a lovely place, Miss Sunderland. Our Patrick did a magnificent job."

"He certainly did. I'm very happy with it, and feel right at home here." She forced herself to smile. All she could think about was not ruining their supper, but she was preoccupied with having to deal with polite conversation.

"Do have a seat, Mr Harkley," she said, indicating one of the comfortable chairs nearby. Instead of sitting, he reached out toward her face.

She leaned back.

His eyes opened wide. "I was not trying to accost you, Miss Sunderland, I promise," he said, clearly offended by her actions. "It's just... you have," he reached out again then grinned.

"You have flour on your cheek."

"Oh!" She grabbed up the apron she'd almost forgotten she wore and tried to remove it.

He stood back trying to stifle a grin, which only made her mad. "Do let me. You're only making it worse. Far worse."

He pulled a clean handkerchief from his pocket and dabbed at her face.

Her heart raced at his nearness. Her mind swirled at the folly of inviting him into her home. She barely knew the man after all. What if...?

No! She wouldn't go there. Nothing would happen – she was perfectly safe with Mr Harkley who was an absolute gentleman.

She stared into his eyes. They seemed to be closer than a few minutes ago. "Is it all gone?" she asked quietly, breaking the silence.

He continued to work on removing the flour. *Exactly how much flour was on her face? It must have been loads.*

He didn't seem inclined to stop, so she took a step back. "I, I need to check on the supper," she said firmly, and headed toward the kitchen.

She heard him follow behind.

"May I help with something?"

His presence was sending her off-balance. Little did she realize when she'd invited him, how much distraction he would be.

She handed him two kitchen towels. "Would you mind pulling the roast out of the oven? It's a little heavy."

Grace admonished herself the moment she'd said the words. They made her sound like a weak female, and she was far from that. "Put it on top of the stove, if you don't mind."

He followed her instructions and Grace checked the meat. It was nearly ready.

"It looks perfect, Miss Sunderland, and smells delicious." He placed the food back in the oven, and Grace pulled the beans further onto the heat.

"Shall we sit while we wait?" She indicated the chair he was meant to sit in earlier, but never did. This time she sat first, hoping he would follow suit.

They stared at each other for long moments, then Mr Harkley spoke. "Thank you again for the invitation, Miss Sunderland." He fiddled with his hands for minute, staring down into his lap.

"Can we drop the formalities? May I call you Grace?"

She glanced up at him, then nibbled on her bottom lip for a moment. Would that be alright? She wasn't certain. "I, I guess it would be alright."

"Then you should call me Joe."

She nodded. "Oh, did I tell you I've finished Mrs Davis's bonnets?"

"No, you didn't. That's great."

Suddenly it the air between them seemed to crackle. Grace jumped up to check the food again. Joe followed.

"It smells really good, Grace," he said. "I haven't had a home cooked meal in a very long time."

She glanced across at him. Surely he ate at home sometimes? "You don't cook?"

He lifted the hot dish out of the oven and placed it on the stove top. "Only if you call canned beans cooking." His face lit up with his smile, and she felt happy inside. "Seriously though, I can cook. I prefer not to spend time cooking for one."

He leaned into the steaming food and breathed deeply. "A man could get used to this," he said as he pulled away.

Grace's heart thudded in her chest. *Exactly what did he mean by that comment?*

She was enjoying his company, that was for sure, but they hardly knew each other. She glanced across at him, but uttered not a word.

"I didn't mean to imply..."

"It's alright," she interrupted. "I didn't take it that way. Besides, I'm not such a great cook." She picked up Aunt Mary's recipe book. "See? Step by step instructions from a dear aunt."

He reached over to take it from her hands. Only instead of the recipe book, one hand wrapped around her much smaller hand.

Her heart rate accelerated, and Grace wasn't sure what to do next. Should she snatch her hand away? Leave it right where it was, or should she simply walk away?

She studied his face – he was also studying hers. "Joe," she said quietly. "The food is ready, I need to serve it."

He continued to stare. Had he even heard her speak? "Would you mind carving the roast?" She gently pulled her hand out of his, and he snapped out of his trance-like state.

"What? Oh, yes, of course."

She placed the vegetables on a platter and began to prepare the gravy while he carved. It felt as though they'd done this before.

A calmness came over Grace, and she wondered what it would be like to be married to Joe. To be his wife, and have this scenario play out day after day.

She stared into the baking dish and quickly stirred the gravy. It was beginning to lump – she hadn't paid enough attention, and was instead daydreaming.

"Darn it," she said quietly, annoyed with herself. She poured a little boiling water into the oven dish until the gravy evened out again, then spooned it into the pretty gravy boat she had waiting nearby.

After the meat was carved, Joe carried it to the table, then returned for the vegetable platter. Grace carried the gravy boat and the plates.

It really did smell delicious. Joe was right – she even surprised herself.

She was about to sit down but jumped up again. "Oh! I need to check the apple pie."

He grabbed her hand as she walked past. "You really are spoiling me, Grace," he said softly, then let go of her hand. He seemed reluctant to do so.

Tonight had been overwhelming already, and it had only just begun. She needed to distance herself from this charismatic man she felt attracted to.

She had long made the decision to be a spinster. Grace wanted a career, her own business. She didn't want to be tied down by a husband and family. She'd made that abundantly clear to her father when he'd told her that was exactly what she would be doing.

He was going to make certain of it. She put a stop to his plans by running away the very next day.

She pulled the apple pie out of the oven and put it aside to cool, then returned to her visitor.

His eyes were on her as she entered the dining room. The moment she sat down, he reached across for her hands.

"Shall we say a prayer of thanks for our food?" he asked quietly.

Grace felt ashamed. She should have realized his intention, but instead thought he had other plans. Not that she would have complained. Not really. She liked it when he touched her.

A shiver went down her spine, and a feeling that she'd never had before entered her whole being. She wasn't sure what any of it meant.

"Please help yourself before the food goes cold," she said when he'd finished speaking.

He began to place food on her plate before his own, and Grace felt humbled. Never before had she seen such a thing. Her father had always served himself first, leaving the leftovers for the women.

She assumed that was normal, but now wondered if she was wrong.

"That is far too much," she said, holding her hand up for him to stop. "I cannot eat anywhere near that amount."

He studied her. "You are far too thin. I think I should fatten you up." He laughed as he said the words, so she took it as a joke.

Joe was very different than what she'd seen before. Perhaps he was more relaxed away from work? Whatever it was, she liked this version of Joe.

She liked the tailor version too, but this one seemed far happier.

He placed two large potatoes on her plate, along with two carrots and some beans. "Enough, please," she said, exasperated. "I simply cannot eat this much food."

She began to remove some of food and he frowned. "I'm not a big eater, I never have been," she said. "But please, help yourself and pile it up. I'd hate for the leftovers to go to waste."

She poured gravy onto her plate, then offered the gravy boat to Joe. She hoped it tasted fine. Of course the night she has a guest has to be the night she messes it up.

Grace sighed.

"It tastes as delicious as it smells," he said, taking a mouthful. "The gravy is perfect too," he said, pulling a face.

She inwardly groaned. It was horrible. The gravy tasted horrid.

She gingerly tasted it. "That was an awful trick you played," she said, pouting. Her gravy was perfect, like the rest of the meal.

He grinned slowly. "I just wanted to stir you up. No one should be so perfect as you." He stared into her eyes, and Grace fought to pull her gaze away, but couldn't.

His hand slid across the table, and gently covered hers. Grace wasn't sure if she should pull it away, or enjoy the warmth of it.

She finally found the fortitude to look away, and glanced down at their entwined hands. "Joe..."

He snatched his hand away. "You're right," he said, looking thoroughly guilty. "I shouldn't presume. It won't happen again."

She nodded and they both went back to their food. The incident was not mentioned again.

Joe lifted the napkin to his lips and Grace watched his every move. "The meal was delicious, Grace. Thank you for inviting me tonight." He placed the napkin on the table, and began to stand. "But I suspect you hadn't intended to ask me."

"I, er,"

He waved his hands about. "It doesn't matter. I think we both enjoyed the evening. Would you like to go for a stroll?"

He glanced at the pile of soiled dishes. "After I help you clean up this mess, of course."

"I would enjoy a stroll. I can tackle these later."

But he would have none of it. "You have been the perfect hostess. Now I shall be the perfect guest." He didn't wait for an answer but poured boiling water into the sink.

Joe rolled up his sleeves and got right into it. The sooner they cleaned up, the sooner he would have the amazing Grace Sunderland on his arm. Her warmth would pour into him, and he would feel whole again.

He closed his eyes. He had to stop having these fantasies about Grace. They had become friends and business acquaintances, and that was the way it should stay.

Besides, he was far from interested in finding a wife.

There was a time he was interested in Emily Stanton, but he had hesitated and she had instead married Patrick Harper. He was over that now. He'd decided it was an infatuation – they'd attended school together, and had spent a lot of time together.

Now that Emily was taken, marriage was totally off his agenda.

But it was nice having Grace around, even if marriage was not on either of their minds.

As Joe passed over the clean dishes, Grace dried them and put them away. Her little kitchen was almost back to normal. Soon they could embark on their stroll around town.

"Tell me," Joe said as they entered the main street. "What are your long-term plans?"

She frowned as she turned to face him. "Long-term? My store is my long-term plan." She looked forward again.

Surely that couldn't be it? She must have other plans for her future? "You don't want to expand your business? Take on staff?" He turned to look at her then. "Find a wonderful man to marry?"

He grinned at her, but she didn't find it funny. In fact, she snatched her arm away. "What are you suggesting, Mr Harkley?" She stepped back and scowled at him.

"I, I'm suggesting nothing, Grace," he said, wondering what happened to her calling him Joe.

His insolence was probably the cause of that. "I was being silly. Trying to get a reaction from you."

She put her hands to her hips. "Well you certainly got that." She hooked her arm through his again, and they continued their walk. "And just so you know, I have no intention of getting married."

He stared at her. "Not ever?"

"I decided a long time ago to be a spinster. So no, not ever."

A headache was starting to develop. Why would such a charming woman make a ridiculous decision like that?

There was only one reason it could be – she'd had her heart broken.

"What was his name," he asked gently.

"What? Who?" Now she looked totally confused.

"The man who broke your heart. What was his name?"

She stopped walking again and stared at him. Then she scowled. And finally she laughed. "You really have no idea what you're talking about," she said, then reached over and patted his hand.

Warmth flooded him.

"I have never been courted, nor do I wish to be." This time she pouted.

Grace

Never been courted? Well that was just crazy.

In that moment, Joe made it his mission to court the captivating Miss Grace Sunderland.

Chapter Five

Joe collected Grace for church, ensuring he was there before she left home. There was no coffee and biscuits this morning due to the picnic.

Everyone would be rushing about to prepare their picnic luncheon. Joe had theirs ready, as he told Grace he would.

He gingerly knocked on the door, not wanting to rush her, but eager to spend time with her.

The door was flung open, and there stood Grace, resplendent in a fresh gown and a pretty bonnet on her head.

His eyes scanned her from head to toe. "You look nice." He could have kicked himself. She looked more than nice, she was beautiful no matter what she wore.

She could be in tatters for all he cared – she would still be spectacular in his eyes.

She smiled. "Thank you. I didn't want to wear my Sunday best to the picnic. Oh, but you have." She stared at him in dismay. "Should I go and change?"

She stepped aside for him to enter. "I have more than one suit, Grace. If this one is ruined, I can always ask the town tailor to make me another." He winked at her.

That made her smile. He liked it when she smiled, which was nowhere near enough. She grabbed up her reticule and was about to step out of the house when she turned back.

"I almost forgot," she said, taking up a container. "Blueberry muffins – my contribution to the picnic." She pulled a face. "Goodness knows what they taste like, but at least I tried."

He was trying too. Trying to get this young woman enamoured to him. The more time he spent with her, the more fond of her he became.

They wandered down to the livery where Joe had arranged for a buggy. He had once considered buying his own, but for the little use it got, it hadn't been worth the expense. If his courtship with Grace worked out, he may reconsider.

Young Charlie was there today – his father never worked on weekends, in fact rarely worked at all these days – and had the buggy ready. Joe placed the picnic basket, blanket, and the container of muffins in the back, then held Grace by the waist, ready to lift her onto the buggy.

The moment he touched her was one he would never forget. Shivers went down his spine and he stood gazing into her eyes.

She frowned. "Joe, is everything alright?"

She had no idea how much her presence moved him. How much her laughter thrilled him, or how much her touch meant to him.

No, he wasn't alright. He was far from alright, as had been the case since the moment Grace Sunderland had entered his life.

He continued to stare at her, continued to hold her by her dainty waist. Then he did the worst thing he could have possibly done – he gazed at her lips.

"You need help, Mr Harkley?" Charlie's voice shattered all thought of kissing Grace, and Joe knew it had been for the best.

One day he would kiss the lovely Grace, but it wouldn't be here in the livery, amongst the dirt with the horses and their excrement. That would just be too...crass.

Grace deserved better than that.

He glanced across at the teenager, then reached into his pocket. "Here's a little something for you, Charlie," he said quietly. "Not for your father – this is for you."

Charlie's face lit up. Everyone knew Charlie had a hard life. He was treated little better than a slave to his scandalous father, and everyone tried to help him in whatever way they could. "Put it aside for your future, Charlie."

Charlie nodded, but Joe doubted he would build a nest egg. One of these days Bart Smith would keel over and die from the sheer amount of alcohol he consumed.

The man was brutal, but young Charlie was not so young anymore, nor was he a boy any longer. He was almost a grown man. Rumor had it that Charlie had already begun to fight back and had protected his mother on more than one occasion.

Joe had a real respect for him.

He glanced at Grace again. She waited patiently, more patiently than he would have been. Finally he lifted her onto the buggy fighting back thoughts of how good if felt to hold her.

Joe walked to the other side of the buggy and climbed up, then flicked the reins to get the horse moving.

The seat of the buggy was not large, and they were forced to sit close together. Joe didn't complain. He relished the feel of Grace next to him, and if he was truthful, had been looking forward to it all week.

"How many people will be at the picnic?"

Her words brought him out of his revelry. He glanced across at her and the act of merely gazing at her sent his senses into free-fall. "Most of the parishioners attend the picnic. It's a big event."

"Oh. How many have you attended?"

He kept his face forward this time, needing to concentrate on what he was doing. "I've been to most of them."

She didn't say anything for a moment, but he could feel her gaze on him. She eventually spoke. "I've never been to a church picnic. Father wouldn't allow it."

What sort of man was this father of hers? Grace had told her a little about him, especially how he'd tried to force her to marry despite her objections.

The man sounded like a brute.

At least she was able to avoid his clutches. They wouldn't have met if she hadn't.

"We're almost there," he said, trying to change the subject from that of sadness, to something far happier.

The picnic was always held in the same place – in a clearing not far from the Mississippi River, about half an hour out of town by buggy, less by horse.

They didn't picnic close to the river because of the children, but anyone who wanted to could wander down later.

Joe pulled the horse to a slow trot, then parked the buggy behind all the other wagons and buggies.

This was traditionally a day for families, and Grace felt like family to him. He hoped she felt the same.

He helped her down and steadied her before letting go. Her hands held his arms, as though she was afraid she'd fall. He stared down at them.

"I won't let you fall, Grace," he said firmly.

"Of course not," she replied. "I feel safe when I'm around you."

His heart thudded. He didn't want to jump to conclusions but...

She licked her lips, and he reached for her again, pulling her close. "Grace."

His words disappeared from his lips when he brushed them across hers.

Her eyes opened wide, but then closed gently, and she leaned into him. But only for a moment. It was as though she suddenly realized where she was. Or perhaps what she was doing.

She shook herself and stepped out of his arms. "We should join the others," she said abruptly.

He'd pushed her too hard. Moved too quickly, and now... had he lost her? He felt hollow, as though he'd lost something precious that meant the world to him.

In reality, he absolutely had.

Grace went to the back of the buggy and reached for the blanket and muffins. She couldn't quite reach them.

"Here, let me."

Joe's nearness sent a tingle through her. What was it about this man that sent her nerve endings on edge?

When he'd pulled her close against him, she was certain she would faint, she was so excited. And when his lips brushed hers, her heart pounded. She could even hear it in her head.

Was that normal? Did kissing a man cause that to happen?

She wasn't sure if she had been elated or just plain scared.

Once her head cleared and she'd understood what was happening, she'd pulled back. It might have felt nice, and although he set her heart alight, she was not interested in being courted.

She'd told him that – in no uncertain terms – so why did he continue to pursue her?

"Grace! Oh, Grace!" She looked up to see Mrs Baker waving to her, Mrs Davis by her side. Joe mumbled something behind her, but she couldn't make out the words, though she could probably guess.

She waved back.

Looking past Mrs Baker she could see a whole heap of people gathered in the area. They made their way to the picnic area, and she looked about. "This is lovely," she said to Joe, as she clutched his arm.

She felt a little apprehensive. After all, she'd never been here before, and truth be told, if she needed to leave by herself for some reason, she would be stuck.

But Joe was a gentleman. He would never abandon her. Not here or anywhere.

"This looks like a good place to put down our blanket," he said, placing the basket down on the ground and taking the blanket from her hands.

He flicked it open and she sat down. It seemed comfortable enough, but she had no intention of sitting here all day.

She looked up at her escort who was still standing. "Could we go for a walk later?"

"Of course," he said, a smile forming on his mouth. "Would you like to see the Mississippi River? It's through that stand of trees."

He pointed and she could just make out water in the distance.

The voices of children playing drifted into her ears and Grace glanced in the opposite direction. A group of young children were playing Ring a Roses, their mothers close by.

It was nice, this picnic day. She'd had no idea it was like this, and had assumed people just sat around eating then went home.

As apprehensive as she'd been, Grace was pleased Joe had asked her along. She was enjoying being part of a community. She'd never really done that before, but now that she was, it felt good.

Joe grabbed both her hands and pulled her onto her feet. "We have time to go for a quick walk now. Not to the river, but into the forest a bit."

She stared up into his eyes. She'd noticed his blue eyes before, of course, but today she studied them. They were the most striking blue she'd ever seen, and they pierced through to her very soul.

"What are you thinking?" he asked, startling her.

She chewed at her bottom lip. "Nothing."

He laughed. "Is it so bad you can't tell me?"

"It's your eyes," she said quietly. "The blue is so striking – I haven't really noticed them before."

He studied her. "Your eyes are so brown, and I most definitely have noticed them before." He pulled her close. "I've noticed everything about you – how could I not?"

She wasn't sure what she should say to that, so pulled away. "What are you trying to say, Joe? I thought we were just friends?"

He stared into her eyes, then his eyes moved down to her mouth. "We are far from friends in my mind." He lifted his hand to her cheek and caressed it. "At least that's how I wished it was."

She opened her mouth to speak, but was interrupted.

"Good afternoon, Grace, Joe." It was Mrs Baker. Couldn't she see they were in the middle of something important.

"Mrs Baker," Joe said with a nod. "We were just about to go on a walk before luncheon." He hooked his arm through Grace's and they headed off for their stroll.

Chapter Six

The day had been wonderful so far. She'd enjoyed their stroll through the forest but that had come to an abrupt end when a whistle sounded.

"That's everyone being called back for luncheon," he said. "There is a group prayer of thanks, and we eat. After that, our time is our own."

They turned to go back, and not for the first time today, Grace didn't want to be around other people. She enjoyed their alone time, although she knew she shouldn't.

Joe was very special – he made her laugh, and he made her feel safe. He always made her feel things she'd never felt before.

She was leaning over a small bush, smelling the fragrance of the tiny flowers when he'd made the announcement. She straightened and hooked her arm through his.

Grace failed to see what he held in his hands. "These are for you, Grace," he said, holding out a bunch of wildflowers. "They didn't cost a heap of money, but they come from the heart."

What a beautiful thing to say. "Thank you, Joe. I will treasure them." She had to fight to stop a grin from crossing her face.

He grinned and she could no longer fight it. Then he became serious. "I would pay one hundred dollars for flowers for you if it meant you understood how I feel about you."

She suddenly felt light headed and her steps faltered. She didn't want him to feel this way about her. There was no future for Joe with the likes of her. Not to mention she'd made it abundantly clear she was not in the least interested in marriage.

He grabbed her by the arms. "Grace? Are you alright?"

She glanced at him, but quickly looked away. "Your words startled me," she said quietly. "No one has ever said such a thing to me before."

"Has anyone ever felt like this toward you before?" His words cut through her heart. How exactly did he feel? He had hinted plenty of times, but she'd chosen to ignore him.

Perhaps she was misinterpreting his question anyway? "What exactly do you mean by *this*?"

They began to walk again, and she hoped that was the end of it. But it was not to be.

"I think you already know," he whispered.

Did she? Deep in her heart, Grace knew exactly what he meant, but hoped she was wrong. She had always vowed not to marry. She had seen the way Father had treated her mother at times, and was not interested in any of that.

Oh, he hadn't been violent – he'd never harmed her – but Mother was a slave to his whims. He would bellow if he didn't get his way, as he had to Grace when she said she wouldn't marry at his command.

She wasn't willing to live her life like that. She didn't blame her mother, she'd had no other choice. Coming from a family of little means, she had been promised to Grace's father when they were young as payment to his father for an overdue account.

Her mother had been traded like a piece of beef. The thought still left a sour taste in Grace's mouth. She had absolutely no intention of being treated like a piece of cattle as her mother had been.

"Oh there you are!" Mrs Baker came running up to them as they re-entered the picnic area. "Preacher Devon is about to say a prayer of thanks for the food."

She stood to the other side of Joe and hooked her arm through his. As much as Grace liked Mrs Baker, she sometimes wished she would leave them be.

She felt a tinge of regret at her thoughts. Mrs Baker was such a lovely person, and Grace was sure she meant no harm. More likely the total opposite.

"Sit down, children," Preacher Devon instructed, and the children went running back to their parents.

When everyone was quiet and the children were all seated he began. "Heavenly Father, thank you for the food we are about to consume, and for the friends we have gathered here today. Amen."

Amen echoed throughout the clearing.

Joe opened the picnic basket and placed everything on the blanket. He had made an assortment of sandwiches, had whole carrots, as well as some apples. He also had a bottle of water. "It looks lovely," she said, reaching for a package of sandwiches.

They chatted as they ate, enjoying the fresh air and each other's company. The children ate quickly then raced off to play again.

"It's lovely here," Grace said, meaning every word of it.

His hand suddenly covered her own. She stared down at their entwined hands, with a mind to pull her hand away.

But she couldn't do it. Grace liked the feel of Joe's hand on hers. Liked the feeling she got when he was near.

He glanced at her, and she was sure he was wondering how long it would take for her to snatch her hand away.

Instead she covered his hand with her free one.

"Grace," he said softly so the rest of the parishioners wouldn't hear. "I really like you."

She opened her mouth to speak when a familiar voice interrupted. "Hello you two. How is my order going?"

Mrs Davis.

"Good afternoon, Mrs Davis," Joe said, obviously wishing she would leave business to another day. "It is well on track. I have finished three gowns and almost done with the fourth."

He glanced at Grace, then back at their customer. "All your matching bonnets are complete."

"That's wonderful," she said cheerfully. Mrs Davis suddenly left them alone again.

Grace breathed a sigh of relief. "Is she always like this?" she whispered.

"Always. I guess she figures if her husband is paying all this money, she has a right to ask anywhere, anytime." He scrubbed his fingers through his hair. "It can be rather frustrating."

That was the moment she realized he'd pulled his hand away.

She stared at his head, and pointed upwards as she giggled. "Um, your hair is all messed up."

He frowned at her. "Really? Or are you just saying that?"

"Really." He pulled his fingers through his hair again, trying to fix it. She shook her head. "Not working." He had another attempt. "That is far worse," she said, frowning this time.

He continued to fix the mess, but it was beyond redemption. Grace leaned forward. "Here, let me."

Her fingers began to weave their way through his chestnut hair until suddenly his hand reached up and grabbed her wrist.

"You have no idea what you're doing to me, do you?" He stared into her eyes, and pulled her hand down to his mouth where he gently kissed the back of her hand. "When we're married, you can do it as much as you like. But out here, with all these gawkers hanging around enjoying the peep show?"

"Did I do something wrong?" Grace felt disappointment. She thought she was helping.

Joe glanced about. "See all these people? They will be watching us. Every moment, every movement, every touch."

"Wait, what?" His previous words suddenly hit her. "I didn't say I'd marry you!" She was suddenly indignant, and Joe sat there laughing at her.

He leaned forward and kissed her cheek. "I wondered how long it would take before you realized."

He sat there grinning as though his words were not outrageous, and as though she'd agreed to marry him.

The cheek of the man!

She stood up in a huff and scampered away before Joe could stop her.

Joe stared after her – his little joke had backfired. The last thing he expected was for Grace to take off.

By the time he stood, she was out of sight. *Which way did she go?* She didn't know this area at all, and now he was afraid she would get lost.

His heart pounded in his chest. He stared toward the area they'd not long left, but wasn't sure if she'd gone that way or down toward the river.

He ran over to Mrs Baker. "Did you see which way Grace went?" he asked urgently. The woman looked confused.

"But she was just there with you." She pointed toward their picnic blanket. "What did you do, Joe?"

He looked to the ground, feeling like a scolded school boy. "I, I made a joke about getting married."

Mrs Baker stood. "Will you never learn?" She sighed. "We could organize a search party."

"No!" He shocked himself with his outburst. "I mean, thank you, but I'll attempt to find her myself. She surely couldn't have gone far."

He made his way back to the area where he'd picked the wildflowers for her, hoping Grace would go where she knew.

He glanced around as he followed their original path, hoping she hadn't gone far. It wasn't long before he found her sitting on a log, studying her ankle.

Joe wanted to pull his gaze away, but that ankle was far too beautiful and coaxed his eyes to stare. He finally noticed the swelling.

"What happened?" he asked urgently. "Let me see." She quickly dropped her skirts back over her previously bare ankle.

"I, I tripped," she said softly. "I think I've twisted my ankle."

This was all his fault. Him and his silly jokes. But this time it wasn't a joke. He was in love with Grace and wanted to marry her.

It seemed crazy that he should be in love with someone after such a short time, but he was. He couldn't get her out of his mind when they were apart, and wanted to be with her constantly.

And when they touched? His nerve endings went out of control.

The problem was he didn't know if Grace felt the same.

He kneeled down in front of her and her eyes opened wide.

"Don't you dare ask me to marry you!" She was becoming hysterical and all he could do was laugh.

"I won't, I promise. But I do want to check that ankle." He pulled at the bottom of her skirts, but she held on tight to it.

Now he was getting exasperated. "I want to make sure it's not broken," he said quietly, and she lifted her skirts just a little. Barely enough for him to see.

He pulled off her boot and it looked distorted, like it might be broken. Before she could protest, he swooped in and picked her up as she clutched her boot.

"Put me down, I can walk," she demanded. He caused this problem and he would fix it.

"I'm doing no such thing, Grace. If it's broken, walking on it will not only be painful, but will do further damage."

She seemed to accept that because her arms slid around his neck and her head rested on his chest.

He was not going to complain.

Mrs Baker ran to them as they emerged from between the trees. "Oh my goodness, what happened?" She hovered so much Joe could barely walk.

"She might have broken her ankle, but I'm not sure," he said. "Did I see Doc Spencer here earlier?"

"Oh, of course. I'll find him." And in the blink of an eye, Mrs Baker was gone.

Chapter Seven

It had been a long day.

Between Doc Spencer pushing her ankle around and calling for makeshift splints, and the bumpy ride home, Grace was exhausted.

Little did she know when they set out for the church picnic the day would end disastrously like this.

She'd ruined the day for everyone. Especially Joe who had been looking forward to it all week. It was all she could do to keep from crying.

He'd been attentive and had looked after her for the rest of the day, and still was.

"You can take me home now," she said firmly. After being properly attended to at the doctor's surgery in town, he'd taken her to his cottage.

The dwelling was far larger than her own home, having been his parent's home before they'd passed on. It was a three bedroom cottage with a large sitting room and large kitchen.

It seemed a shame that Joe didn't cook when he had such wonderful facilities available. Or was that another one of his jokes?

Sometimes she couldn't tell his jokes from what was real.

Against her better judgement, Grace sat in the sitting room with a cushion behind her back and two pillows under her ankle.

Doc Spencer had supplied her with a set of crutches that she would need to use for at least a few days.

She sighed.

The worst part was this injury was self-inflicted. If she hadn't run away from Joe and his heartfelt words, this would never have happened.

And what of her business? It hadn't even had a chance to become established and she had to abandon it.

"What is going on in that pretty little head?" Joe asked. He stood in the doorway watching her every move, a mug of tea in his hands.

She sighed again. "Far too much, I'm afraid."

He placed the tea on the side table, then sat down in a nearby chair.

"Talk to me – tell me what is worrying you." She stared into his face. Concern was written all over it.

Grace squeezed her eyes tight. "What about my business? How does it run without me? I might as well close down." A tear trickled slowly down her cheek and he brushed it away with his thumb.

The action sent a shudder rippling through her.

"It's all my fault," he said, studying her. "If I hadn't joked about getting married, you wouldn't have run off."

"Only it wasn't a joke." She said the words quietly and watched closely for his reaction.

He shook his head. "No, it wasn't. I'm really sorry, Grace." He reached over and took both her hands in his. "I do want to marry you. I care for you – a lot."

He leaned in and kissed her cheek. "I'll do whatever I can to help."

"You don't have to do anything. It's my fault. I'm the one who ran off."

He stood and began to leave the room. "I have to prepare the spare bed for tonight. I'll be back shortly."

"What? No!" She glared at him. "I can't sleep here in the same house as you!"

He turned back to face her. "There's no choice. Doc Spencer said you'll need help for at least couple of days before you can be alone." He shrugged his shoulders. "I'm sorry, Grace. That sprained ankle is going to take some time to heal."

He left her alone and Grace tried to stop her thoughts from overtaking rational thinking. Foremost on her mind was the fact they would be under the one roof with no chaperone. And they weren't married.

Her reputation would be in tatters.

Did that mean Joe would get his way? Would she be forced to marry him because of this situation?

She really liked Joe, but didn't want to be forced into marriage with him, as much as he wanted to marry her.

She could hear him whistling. *Did that mean he was happy about their predicament?* She felt annoyance building up inside her.

"Your room is ready," he called as he returned to the sitting room. "Do you want to rest now?"

"What I want, is to go home," she said between clenched teeth.

She began to stand and almost toppled over. "Easy." He grabbed her arms before she could fall. "This is exactly why you have to stay here for a few nights at least."

She reluctantly nodded her agreement – what else could she do? It was clear she wouldn't be able to care for herself, at least until she mastered the crutches.

His hands slid beneath her and he carried her to the spare room. It wasn't tiny but wasn't overly large either. The windows were covered with lace curtains, and there was a pretty upholstered chair in the corner.

Next to the bed sat a three drawer cupboard with a runner and lantern on top. The eiderdown was made with a pretty flower pattern and looked perfect in this room.

Grace decided Joe's mother had furnished the room – it was far too feminine for him to have designed it.

"Do you like it?" His voice came out of nowhere and startled her back to the present.

She turned to him and smiled. "I do, I really do. Your mother's handiwork?"

"Yes, she furnished the entire cottage. It was something she loved to do." He sighed.

Grace looked up at him. "You obviously miss her."

"I do. I miss them both."

He carried her to the bed and placed her gently on top. "I'll bring your tea in here, and if you feel like it, you can have a nap."

Joe sat down on the bed and took both her hands. "I'm truly sorry, Grace. I never meant for any of this to happen." He opened his mouth as though to say something else but didn't.

He returned shortly with her tea, then left her alone. It didn't take long before Grace fell asleep.

* * *

Grace awoke to movement not far away, and could hear the low murmur of voices. The aroma of food drifted into her senses, and it made her realize she was hungry.

Moments later Joe was standing in the doorway watching her. "Did you have a good nap?" He looked rather amused, though what he found funny, she had no idea. "Supper is ready."

She pushed back the eiderdown that she'd climbed under earlier, and began to get out of bed but the crutches were nowhere to be seen. "Let me," he said scooping her up and not giving her the opportunity to refuse.

He carried her out to the dining room table, where a delicious looking meal had been served. Three settings were laid out, which confused her.

"Hello Grace." Mrs Baker was in the kitchen, organizing the food. "I hope you're hungry."

"Oh, hello Mrs Baker."

Joe helped her onto a chair, then explained. "Mrs Baker kindly made supper for us. She'll be staying the night too."

Relief overwhelmed her, and she let out a huge sigh.

"What? You didn't honestly think I would put your reputation at stake, did you?" He looked truly offended. "Of course I had to organize a chaperone, and Mrs Baker offered to do it."

She reached out her hand to him. "Thank you, Joe. I really appreciate it."

"Ah, Grace," Mrs Baker said. "How is the ankle doing?" She placed a platter of vegetables on the table, then began to serve out the chicken.

"It's a little better than before. Thanks for asking."

"Eat – both of you eat up before it gets cold."

The meal was eaten in near silence, but the one thing weighing heavy on her mind was now rectified.

"When can I go home," Grace asked after they finished the meal. She didn't want to appear too anxious, but she was certainly feeling that way.

Joe held both her hands. "Doc says a couple of days at least. You can't leave until you can walk by yourself. Even if that means with the crutches."

She glanced down at their entwined hands. "Then I guess I have no choice."

He lifted her chin so she faced him. "Will it be so bad to stay here a few nights?"

"I don't want to be an imposition. Besides, I'll get bored."

He glanced across at Mrs Baker, then back to Grace. "You are not an imposition. What are friends for?"

"But..."

"It's already arranged. Mrs Baker will stay with you until she needs to open the diner. If I didn't have this order for Mrs Davis, I'd stay with you myself."

"This is far too much trouble for the likes of me."

She heard the collective gasp from her two companions.

"Grace," Joe said quietly. "You are worth the extra effort. I don't think you realize how special you are." He leaned in and gently kissed her cheek.

"I second that," Mrs Baker said. "Now let's not have any such talk again." She began to clear the dishes and left Grace and Joe alone.

Joe pulled his chair closer to hers, and held both her hands. "I know life has been tough," he said quietly. "And I know you've lost a lot. Please don't ever downplay your importance." He leaned closer and she rested her head on his chest.

"It hasn't been long since you came to Grand Falls, and already you've been accepted by everyone." He leaned back to look into her face. "We all love you, Grace." His voice broke as he said the words, and her heart thudded in her chest.

"I am overwhelmed by your kindness," she said quietly. "By everyone's kindness." She glanced toward the kitchen, feeling helpless watching Mrs Baker clearing up the mess. She should be helping but was incapable right now.

"Apart from your injury, did you enjoy the picnic?"

She managed a small smile. "I did enjoy it. Perhaps next time we'll get to stroll along the river."

For the first time tonight he grinned at her. "We can arrange that. But you need to heal first." He suddenly stood, then swooped in and picked her up, placing her in the sitting room, her ankle propped up with pillows.

"I'll be back shortly. Tea or coffee?"

"I prefer tea, but you don't have to fuss..."

"It's no bother." Then he was gone.

Chapter Eight

Joe had begun work early. He wanted to get this order finished as quickly as he could so he could look after Grace himself.

She was an exquisite flower that needed extra care, and he wanted to be the one to do that. He was more than grateful for Mrs Baker's help, but if Grace was to be his wife, then she was his responsibility.

He was certain she had no idea of his depth of love for her. What could he do to prove it?

That was something he needed to think on. For now, he needed to finish this gown and begin work on the next. Only two to go, and at this rate he'd be finished by noon tomorrow.

He leaned back in relief. Moments later, the bell over the door tinkled. He looked up to see Mrs Davis standing there.

"Good morning Mrs Davis. What can I do for you today?"

She was always a picture of perfection, and was the nicest woman. Her husband was nice too, but he was pedantic when it came to his wife's appearance.

"I came to ask if it would be possible to take whatever is ready now, Mr Harkley."

He wondered how long it would take.

"I have a function to attend to tonight, and it would be wonderful to be able to wear one of my new outfits." She smiled appreciatively. He never could resist this gracious lady.

"Three of the gowns are totally ready, and the others should be finished by noon tomorrow." He scratched his head. "Unfortunately the bonnets are locked up in Grace's store. Otherwise I could give you those too."

She waved her hands about. "My dear boy," she always called him a boy. Did she not realize he had now passed his thirtieth birthday? "Surely you could ask Grace for the keys to retrieve my bonnets?" She pleaded to him with her eyes. She always did that when she wanted to get her own way.

"Of course I shall try. I'll visit with Grace in the luncheon break. Hopefully it won't be a problem."

Now she looked stern. "I'll return at three. That should give you enough time to retrieve my bonnets and have the three gowns packaged."

"But Mrs Davis," he said, feeling worried now. "I always deliver your gowns to your door."

She brushed his concern aside. "This is not your fault, Mr Harkley. Mr Davis forget to mention this function, hence the rush. I'll have my driver bring me back at three and all will be well." She turned toward the entrance. "Goodbye Mr Harkley."

As quickly as she had arrived, she was gone.

This put a whole new perspective on his day. He prepared the garment steamer for when he was done, then sat back down at his machine and worked at finishing the gown in front of him. It wouldn't take much longer.

His mind had strayed to Grace more than a few times this morning, otherwise this gown would already be finished.

He put the finishing touches on the gown, then clipped all the stray pieces of cotton. Four gowns completed.

He prepared the cardboard boxes, then began to steam the gowns. They were his best yet, and he was convinced Mrs Davis would adore them.

Joe folded each gown carefully, and added a handwritten thank you card to each box, as was his practice. The little touches kept his customers coming back.

He closed the lid on the last box, then turned the sign on his door. *Back in one hour.*

Hopefully that would be enough time. He was yet to find out.

* * *

He had always planned to eat at home today – the more time he got to spend with Grace the better – but because of the circumstances, it was a rush. Grace sat at the table with him, and they both had sandwiches Mrs Baker had prepared earlier.

"I'll walk back with you when you leave, Mr Harkley," she said then glanced at Grace. "Are you sure you'll be alright by yourself this afternoon?"

Grace finished what was in her mouth before answering. "I will, I promise. I am so grateful to both of you for all you've done." She took a sip of tea, then glanced at Joe. "I'm fine to go back home now."

He laughed. "Nice try. Maybe in a couple of days." Joe took a large gulp of coffee. "Doc Spencer wants to check your injury before you go – just to be sure it's healing properly."

He began to stand. "I have to go shortly if you're nearly ready, Mrs Baker."

The older woman nodded. "Whenever you are."

He kissed Grace on the cheek before he left, fully aware he would have kissed her lips if Mrs Baker hadn't been there. He was certain Grace had feelings for him – all he had to do now was get her to admit it.

Grace had supplied him with the keys to the store, and told him where to find the bonnets. More than once she told him how grateful she was to him for helping her out, and how relieved she was to have finished her order early.

As the pair strolled back toward town, he didn't talk much. He was too busy thinking of ways to get Grace to admit to her feelings.

She was a stubborn woman for sure. She'd made a decision never to marry, and decided to stick to it, no matter the consequences.

"There's no doubt about it, you have to find a way into her heart." Mrs Baker stared at him. "You just have to work out what is going to do that."

That wasn't news. Joe already knew that. "That's the hardest part. Grace likes to keep to herself. You've seen what she's like, she doesn't give much away."

Mrs Baker headed toward the diner as Joe headed toward *Graceful Bonnets*. "Good luck with it."

"I'll need far more than luck," he muttered as he turned the key to Grace's store. He went inside, and following her instructions, located the boxes of bonnets. Mrs Davis would be beyond happy with this result.

As he leaned in to pick up the boxes in the darkened room, he knocked something over on the storage counter. He picked it up to set it right again, only to discover it was a framed photograph.

He took it into the store where the light was better. It was a photograph of Grace with her beloved cat, Grumps. Joe knew how much she missed her feline companion – she had mentioned it several times.

He stared down into the photograph – they looked so happy, and his heart broke. He wished there was something he could do to help. But what could he do?

He set the photograph back where it belonged and took the hat boxes. There was still heaps of time until three, but knowing his best customer, she would arrive early.

Joe locked the door and hurried back to his own store, ready to match the bonnets with the gowns before Mrs Davis arrived.

He opened each box, for both the gowns and bonnets, and matched them up, sitting the hat boxes on top of the corresponding gown.

The bonnets were stunning, each one beautifully crafted, and each unique. He knew Mrs Davis would be ecstatic.

"Wonderful!" She clapped her hands as she entered the store, spotting the hat boxes. "Thank you, Mr Harkley – I knew you could do it."

As predicted, she was over an hour early.

She rushed over to the counter to study her purchases. She opened the first hat box and pulled out the bonnet. "Oh my, this is magnificent." She pulled it on her head and stared in the full-length mirror. "Tell Miss Sunderland I am extremely impressed," she said after studying her reflection for a full two minutes.

She handed it back to Joe who placed it back in its box. Then she opened the next box and tried the bonnet on, then the next, and the next. "That young woman is extremely creative," she finally said, handing the last bonnet back to Joe. "I hope your gowns are just as good," she said jokingly.

He grinned. "Of course, Mrs Davis. You wouldn't expect anything less."

She laughed, which was exactly what he expected. "How is the dear girl fairing? Is the ankle healing?"

"It is, Mrs Davis. She should be able to return home in a day or two." He lifted some of the boxes and carried them out to her carriage.

"Thank you, Mr Harkley," she said. "You have helped me out of a tight spot." She shoved some notes into his hands, but he handed them back.

"Please, Mrs Davis. Your husband pays handsomely for my services. I couldn't take another penny." She looked shocked at his refusal. "But there is something you might be able to do for me."

She leaned in and listened carefully to what he said, then nodded, a grin on her face.

"This is going to be so much fun," she said, then Joe helped her into the carriage. He stared after her as the carriage disappeared down the road.

Now, if his plan worked, he'll be a very happy man.

Chapter Nine

"You have no idea how relieved I am to be back home."

Joe helped her into a comfortable chair and took the crutches. "Don't forget what Doc Spencer said – you need to continue using the crutches until your ankle has completely healed."

She pouted. "I know, but that doesn't mean I like it."

"And you're to rest that ankle until next week. That means no work."

Since when did that matter? Her business was going nowhere. With the store closed for days on end while she was at Joe's place, customers couldn't even buy her ready-made bonnets.

She sighed.

"Yes, Joe, I'll do what the doctor said." He grinned, but fully understood she would do no such thing. The moment his back was turned she would be out in the store working.

Totally against medical advice.

"Promise me you'll at least wait to open the store until tomorrow." He pleaded with her, but wasn't convinced it would work.

She grimaced. "What makes you think I would do that?"

He felt like laughing. He knew her too well. "Oh nothing. Perhaps your streak of stubbornness?" He kneeled down in front of her and took both her hands. "Please, Grace. Rest for the remainder of the day at least. I'll come back and check on you in a little while."

He leaned in and lightly kissed her lips. She didn't pull back, and didn't push him away. The connection felt... good.

Joe had longed to kiss her like this for so long.

It was time to go. He had to open his own store now, as he had customers arriving to collect their orders.

"Joe," she said quietly as he began to stand. Her arms wrapped around his neck and she pulled him closer. Without warning she kissed him.

His heart was pounding, and his head was spinning. Was Grace finally warming to him? Had she finally given in to her feelings instead of her resolve to be a spinster forever?

He had no idea and didn't care. All that mattered now was that the delectable Miss Grace Sunderland was kissing him.

His arms snaked up around her back and he held her tight. "Grace," he whispered. "Are you sure this is what you want?"

She rested her head on his shoulder and his heart thudded in his chest. Why did he ask? This is what he'd wanted all along, but she'd held back, had been reluctant to get close to him.

He heard her sigh.

Joe suddenly felt hollow. Was she going to deny him her warmth, her closeness? He prayed she didn't.

Finally, she pulled away. His heart broke.

"I..." She glanced at him, then licked her lips. "Why don't you sit down? You're making me nervous?"

Nervous? That really wasn't a good sign. Was it?

He did as he was told, pulling the chair closer.

She leaned forward, and he did the same until they were so close their lips almost met. It was unsettling, and Joe leaned back.

"I'm not sure how to say this," she began, and he felt even more hollow than before. She was about to say the words he dreaded to hear. "I was wrong."

Grace leaned back in the chair, not saying another word.

"Wrong? About what?" Now he was totally confused. He thought she was breaking up with him. Not that they were ever together, not really.

She licked her lips and his eyes followed every movement. It took all his effort not to reach out and pull her to him and kiss her tenderly.

No, that wasn't true. The time for tenderness was gone – this woman stirred up the passion in him. He sighed inwardly as he studied her.

"I thought I wanted to be a spinster." Hope enveloped his heart. Was she saying what he thought she was saying?

"And now?"

"And now I don't." His heartbeat quickened, his hands began to sweat, and Joe was elated.

He forced himself to calm down, he might be totally misinterpreting her words. "And what does that mean exactly?" Should he dare to hope?

"It means, Joe, that I agree to allowing you to court me."

Before he could stop himself, Joe jumped out of his chair and pulled her up into his arms. His arms went around her and up her back, and he kissed Grace like he'd never kissed before.

Until he heard her groan. Her ankle! He'd totally forgotten about her ankle.

He swooped her up into his arms, and kissed her again.

* * *

It had been a week since Grace had made her announcement to Joe, and she felt good about it.

Her ankle was almost back to normal, and she no longer needed the crutches. He was collecting her for a stroll this afternoon. She'd told him she felt ready – for a short stroll at least.

It had been so long, and one thing she loved to do was go for walks. He'd promised to take her down to the riverside as soon as she felt strong enough. She was looking forward to it.

Grace readied herself for Joe's visit. She'd rested her ankle all day to ensure she wouldn't falter on their venture outside. She couldn't wait.

She was finishing up the dishes when there was a knock at the door. "Coming." She didn't rush, and took her time. Doc Spencer told her to take it easy in case she caused a relapse. That was the last thing she wanted to do.

Opening the door, she fully expected to see Joe, and there he was, standing in front of her with a grin on his face. He leaned in and kissed her cheek, and she opened the door wider.

It was then she noticed the large box in his hands. "What do you have there?"

He ushered her inside. "It's a surprise."

She couldn't help but grin. Grace loved surprises. Perhaps that was because it was such a rare occurrence.

"Sit down and you can open it."

She did as he said and Joe put the box on her lap, keeping his grip on it. "Is it breakable?" Her eyes were wide and she was beyond excited.

"It certainly is. Do you like surprises?"

"I love surprises." He would tuck that information in the back of his mind for future reference, but knew nothing would out shine this surprise.

She glanced up at him. "Should I open it now?"

The box moved slightly, and he held it tighter. She stared at him. "Did that box just move?"

"Perhaps," he said, "You should hurry up and open it in case I drop it." He wasn't giving anything away.

Her fingers flew to the lid and she began to open it but stopped when she heard a muffled sound. "Oh!"

"Open it, Grace. I know you'll love it – no need to be scared."

She gingerly lifted the lid and her eyes filled with tears. "Oh, Joe. It's beautiful," she said, tears trickling down her face. He wiped them away with his thumb. "What a dear little creature. So precious."

She pulled the kitten out of the box and held it close. "You are an extraordinary man," she said. "It is the best surprise I've ever had."

The kitten rubbed itself against her chin. "Does it have a name? Where did you get it? Oh, we'll have to get a bed for it, and..."

"No, it doesn't have a name. I got her from Mrs Davis, and what was the last question? Oh, the bed? Already done."

He retrieved the box he'd left outside the door with the kitten's supplies – bedding, bowls, and enough food to keep Grace going for at least a few days.

She stared at the kitten for long moments, and his heart felt happy. If she hadn't sprained her ankle, this idea would never have come to him. He'd heard Mrs Davis had a litter of kittens out on their property, so it worked perfectly.

He'd had to wait until Grace was capable of looking after herself before introducing a needy kitten into her life. It had taken all his resolve not to give the surprise away.

Grace stood with the kitten still in her arms and hugged him. "Thank you," she whispered. "You are always thinking of ways to make me happy. It is just one of the reasons I love you."

She loves him? She loves him!

"I love you too, Grace, more than you could ever imagine. I knew this sweet ball of white fluff with little black boots on its feet would make you happy."

"Boots! I'm going to call her boots."

She hugged him again, and Joe knew with all his heart Grace would finally agree to marry him.

Chapter Ten

Grace was a bundle of nerves.

Joe had delivered her new gown yesterday, with instructions not to open the box until the next day.

Her two friends, Mrs Baker and Mrs Davis were there, helping her. Little Boots mewed as she wandered around.

After three months, she had finally settled in, and was growing. Grace enjoyed having a kitten again. She still missed Grumps, but Boots had repaired the hole in her heart.

Joe had finally admitted the photograph had given him the idea. She didn't care how the idea had come to him, she was just grateful for her new companion.

"You've been in that bath long enough, Grace," Mrs Baker yelled through the door. "It's time to get out before you shrink."

She was right. Grace had been in the bath for far too long. Her skin was beginning to pucker up, and that just wouldn't do.

"Don't you open the box yet," she called. She didn't want those two sweet ladies opening the dress box without her there. Joe had said it was a special surprise, and he knew how much she loved surprises.

She climbed out of the bath and dried herself off. She was so grateful for the modern plumbing Patrick had arranged for her when he'd built her residence.

She dried her hair as best she could, and hoped it would dry in time.

Those sweet ladies out there in her sitting room were beginning to worry. Or perhaps panic was a better word.

Wasn't it traditional for the bride to be late for her wedding?

Her thoughts turned to Joe. What would he be doing now? He was a stickler for punctuality, so he was probably already on his way to the church.

No doubt he would drive Preacher Devon crazy once he arrived.

She strode out into her bedroom in her undergarments and wrapped up in a big white towel. The ladies were there waiting.

"*Now* can we open the box?" They both asked at the same time.

Grace sat on the side of the bed and glanced up at them. She was more nervous to see her wedding gown than she'd ever been before.

Joe wouldn't let her see even a glimpse of it.

Grace swallowed, then lifted the lid to the box. On top was a notecard from Joe. But it wasn't like those he normally wrote.

I love you more than life itself. I can't wait for us to be husband and wife.

He drew a little heart underneath.

Tears trickled down Grace's face at reading his words.

"Well," Mrs Davis said with false indignation, "He never writes things like that to me!" They all laughed.

Grace wiped at her tears and reached for the gown, then gently laid it across the bed.

The three women stood staring down at it.

"He has outdone himself this time," Mrs Davis said.

Mrs Baker added, "The man is a magician with a sewing machine."

Grace was speechless and her eyes filled with tears again, overwhelmed by the beauty of her wedding gown – it had a silk underlay, and was made mostly of lace on the top.

She still couldn't believe she was getting married today.

Mrs Baker suddenly disappeared, and quickly returned with a wet face cloth. "Here, put this on your eyes. We can't have you walking down the aisle with red, puffy eyes." She handed the cloth to Grace. "What would Joe say?"

"He'd probably say he didn't care," Mrs Davis said. "Provided he got to marry his beautiful Grace."

Grace lay down on the bed and placed the cloth over her eyes. It was hard to believe that in less than an hour she'd been a married woman.

It was even harder to believe she had fallen in love, and with such a wonderful, caring man.

* * *

Grace stood at the back of the church.

He could see she was nervous, but oh Lord, she looked magnificent. He had spent the better part of two weeks designing and making her gown.

He'd had to order far more lace than he'd ever used on any other project. He vowed it would be his best creation yet, and it was.

There was no way he would ask Grace to make her own wedding bonnet, so he made that too. He had never made a bonnet before, and it wasn't easy. He'd had to send away for a pattern. Imagine that – *Graceful Bonnets* stood less than fifteen yards across the way, and he couldn't ask Grace for a pattern.

That would have spoiled the surprise.

She held a bouquet of fresh flowers in her hands – white carnations to go along with her white dress. He chuckled to himself – he would not have been at all surprised to see her enter the church with Boots in her hands instead of a bouquet. Those two were inseparable.

Grace was a picture of perfection, and in a few minutes they would be joined together in marriage. Forever.

Joe couldn't believe how fortunate he'd been in meeting Grace. Or how fortunate he'd been with her choosing Grand Falls to set up her new business.

He grinned at her surprise at having her father come out of nowhere to walk her down the aisle. George Sunderland had been pleasantly surprised to receive Joe's letter, and of course he and his wife wanted to be at their daughter's wedding. He promised he had changed his tyrannical ways.

He thought he would never outshine Boots as a surprise, but this would be his best surprise yet. Joe vowed to make this her best day ever, and hoped that's what he'd done.

Glancing up, he saw the surprise on Grace's face at her father's presence, and the two hugged each other. Then Meredith, her mother, joined them.

He watched as Grace wiped the tears from her eyes, but her smile was a mile wide. He automatically knew Mrs Baker and Mrs Davis, who had kept his surprise secret, would be having conniptions over her tears.

Her parents placed themselves either side of their only daughter and they all prepared to make their way down to Joe and Preacher Devon.

It seemed to take a lifetime, but when they finally arrived, her father handed Grace over to him. Joe held both of her hands tightly. There was no way he was letting go now that he'd got her into the church.

The preacher glanced at Joe. "Ready?"

He was more than ready – he wanted to be married to the love of his life. "Absolutely," he said.

"What about you, Grace," Preacher Devon asked.

She wiped another stray tear, and Joe caressed her cheek. "I'm ready too."

The preacher leaned forward and whispered. "Then let's get this ceremony started."

And that's exactly what he did. "Dearly beloved, we are gathered here today..."

When they were finally pronounced husband and wife, Joe turned to his new wife. "I love you," he said quietly, then leaned in and kissed her. He didn't want to stop, but knew he must.

After all the paperwork was done, and he held the marriage certificate in his hand, Joe was beyond ecstatic. Grace was finally his wife, and they could begin their new life together.

He held her hand firmly as they walked back down the aisle and out the door. Soon everyone was outside throwing rice at them.

Joe decided it was more rice than he'd seen in his entire life.

Epilogue

Two years later...

"You really need to slow down, Grace."

She brushed Joe's words aside. "Let me finish these last few bonnets and I'll stop, I promise."

She looked exhausted and he was exasperated with her. Their second baby was due in a few days, and he couldn't get her to stop working.

Her parents had recently moved into Grace's little residence – they wanted to be closer to Grace and their grandchildren, which he could fully understand.

Of course he offered for them to move in to the family home, but they would have none of it. Joe was not displeased.

Besides, it was a good deterrent for potential robbers to steer clear of *Graceful Bonnets* having them there.

"Honestly," he said, "I don't even know how you still fit behind the sewing machine." He stared down at her. "I think it's time we thought about getting someone in for you to train. With two children, it's not going to be easy for you to continue.

She looked truly dismayed. "But I love making bonnets," she said, her bottom lip wobbling.

"Are they orders?" If they were, he'd tackle them. Grace was in no position to be sewing at this point in her pregnancy.

"No, but..."

He reached out for her hands. "Grace," he said gently. "Please stop." She looked ready to collapse with exhaustion. If it hadn't been for her mother, he wouldn't know Grace was working – she was meant to be home resting.

Joe helped her to her feet. "No, no, no!" she screamed as her waters broke. "Not yet, not now."

"I'll go get the Doc," George Sunderland said urgently.

"I'll take her home," Joe said. He turned to Grace's mother. "Meredith, can you please look after little Henry?"

He was surprised at how calm he was, considering the panic he went into when Henry was born. But second time around it wasn't as bad.

At least he didn't think it was. Not yet anyway.

Their home wasn't far, so he carried her. There was no way he was letting her walk.

Doc Spencer arrived with his wife around the same time they did, and everything was prepared. Meredith and George came soon after with young Henry, Joe's little apprentice as he called him.

One day he *would* be Joe's apprentice, and nothing would make him prouder. He could picture the sign on the door already – *Joseph Harkley & Son*

He sighed. It was a long way off, and he had to concentrate on the task at hand. Grace and their new baby.

Meredith handed Henry to him, then shoo'd the men out of the house, except the Doc of course.

This was the part he hated. Being banished from his wife's side. He didn't want to lose her, and it was agony waiting outside, hearing her screams, not knowing what was going on.

But he did as he was ordered, and they paced the street. They had to go far enough away that young Henry couldn't hear his mother's agonizing screams.

They decided to go to the diner instead. Mrs Baker looked after them well, especially little Henry, whom she adored.

Joe took a few sips of his coffee, then paced the room. "Oh for goodness sakes, Joe, sit down." Mrs Baker practically ordered him.

He did as he was told and took a few more sips, then paced the floor again. This time she stared at him and shook her head.

Two hours later Meredith ran through the door to fetch them. Joe stared at her. Only two hours? Something must be terribly wrong, and his heart thudded in his chest.

"Is she...? He couldn't say the words.

Meredith grinned. "Grace is perfectly fine, and so is baby Alice. My daughter is just as stubborn as she always was." She walked toward him and reached out her arms to hug him. "She's been in labor all day but didn't tell anyone."

He should have expected nothing less. This *was* Grace they were talking about.

"Come on, Henry. Time to meet your baby sister." Joe leaned down and picked the boy up. George and Meredith joined them.

By the time they arrived back at the house, Doc Spencer had finished everything he needed to do. Joe went in first, Henry stayed with his grandparents. He sat on the edge of the bed, and studied Grace, then their new baby daughter.

"She's beautiful like her mother," he said quietly as she breastfed their newborn. "She has your blonde hair too."

He leaned in and hugged them both, knowing he was the luckiest man in the world. He had a perfect family and a perfect life.

"Baby." Little Henry came running in, his little legs couldn't get there fast enough. "Baby," he repeated, his arms outstretched.

"Meet your new baby sister," Joe told him as he picked the toddler up. "This is Alice."

Henry leaned in and kissed his little sister. "Baby play."

Grace and Joe both laughed. It would be a long time before Alice would be able to play. They hugged their beautiful family, and Joe said a silent prayer of thanks to God for sending Grace to him.

"Reow." They all turned their heads at the fluffy white interloper.

"Boots!" Henry wriggled until his father let him on the floor to play with their wonderful feline who was well entrenched in their family.

His family was complete, but Joe would never be unhappy if it happened to grow a little more.

From the Author

Thank you for reading *Grace*! I hope you enjoyed Grace and Joe's story as much as I enjoyed writing it. The *Brides of Montana* series continues with *Victoria*.

Books in this series are as follows:

Emily

Grace

Victoria

Maggie

Callie

Olivia

To find out about new books, sign up for my newsletter at:

cheryl-wright.com/newsletter/

About the Author

Multi-published, award-winning and bestselling author Cheryl Wright, former secretary, debt collector, account manager, writing coach, and shopping tour hostess, loves reading.

She writes both historical and contemporary western romance, as well as romantic suspense.

She lives in Melbourne, Australia, and is married with two adult children and has six grandchildren. When she's not writing, she can be found in her craft room making greeting cards.

Links

Website: *http://www.cheryl-wright.com/*

Facebook Reader Group:
https://www.facebook.com/groups/cherylwrightauthor/

Join My Newsletter:

https://cheryl-wright.com/newsletter/